1935 if you wanted to
read a good book, you needed
either a lot of money or a library card.
Cheap paperbacks were available, but their
poor production generally mirrored the quality
between the covers. One weekend that year,
Allen Lane, Managing Director of The Bodley Head,
having spent the weekend visiting Agatha Christie,
found himself on a platform at Exeter station trying to
find something to read for his journey back to London.
He was appalled by the quality of the material he had to
choose from. Everything that Allen Lane achieved from that
day until his death in 1970 was based on a passionate belief
in the existence of 'a vast reading public for *intelligent*
books at a low price'. The result of his momentous vision
was the birth not only of Penguin, but of the 'paperback
revolution'. Quality writing became available for the price of
a packet of cigarettes, literature became a mass medium
for the first time, a nation of book-borrowers became a
nation of book-buyers – and the very concept of book
publishing was changed for ever. Those founding
principles – of quality and value, with an overarching
belief in the fundamental importance of reading –
have guided everything the company has
done since 1935. Sir Allen Lane's
pioneering spirit is still very much alive
at Penguin in 2005. Here's to
the next 70 years!

MORE THAN A BUSINESS

'We decided it was time to end the almost customary half-hearted manner in which cheap editions were produced – as though the only people who could possibly want cheap editions must belong to a lower order of intelligence. We, however, believed in the existence in this country of a vast reading public for intelligent books at a low price, and staked everything on it'
Sir Allen Lane, 1902–1970

'The Penguin Books are splendid value for sixpence, so splendid that if other publishers had any sense they would combine against them and suppress them'
George Orwell

'More than a business ... a national cultural asset'
Guardian

'When you look at the whole Penguin achievement you know that it constitutes, in action, one of the more democratic successes of our recent social history'
Richard Hoggart

Rose, 1944

HELEN DUNMORE

PENGUIN BOOKS

PENGUIN BOOKS

Published by the Penguin Group
Penguin Books Ltd, 80 Strand, London WC2R 0RL, England
Penguin Group (USA) Inc., 375 Hudson Street, New York, New York 10014, USA
Penguin Group (Canada), 10 Alcorn Avenue, Toronto, Ontario, Canada M4V 3B2
(a division of Pearson Penguin Canada Inc.)
Penguin Ireland, 25 St Stephen's Green, Dublin 2, Ireland
(a division of Penguin Books Ltd)
Penguin Group (Australia), 250 Camberwell Road, Camberwell, Victoria 3124,
Australia (a division of Pearson Australia Group Pty Ltd)
Penguin Books India Pvt Ltd, 11 Community Centre,
Panchsheel Park, New Delhi – 110 017, India
Penguin Group (NZ), cnr Airborne and Rosedale Roads, Albany,
Auckland 1310, New Zealand (a division of Pearson New Zealand Ltd)
Penguin Books (South Africa) (Pty) Ltd, 24 Sturdee Avenue,
Rosebank 2196, South Africa

Penguin Books Ltd, Registered Offices: 80 Strand, London WC2R 0RL, England

www.penguin.com

Rose, 1944, Whales and Seals, Esther to Fanny previously unpublished
Annina first published in *Love of Fat Men* by Viking 1997
First published in Penguin Books 1998
This selection first published as a Pocket Penguin 2005

1

Copyright © Helen Dunmore, 1997, 2005
All rights reserved

The moral right of the author has been asserted

Set in 11/13pt Monotype Dante
Typeset by Palimpsest Book Production Limited
Polmont, Stirlingshire
Printed in England by Clays Ltd, St Ives plc

Except in the United States of America, this book is sold subject
to the condition that it shall not, by way of trade or otherwise, be lent,
re-sold, hired out, or otherwise circulated without the publisher's
prior consent in any form of binding or cover other than that in
which it is published and without a similar condition including this
condition being imposed on the subsequent purchaser

Contents

Rose, 1944

If she shuts her eyes and counts to twenty she'll feel him before she sees him. His hand on her bare neck.

'I been everywhere lookin for you, Rose.'

He likes her name. He likes to say it and hold it in his mouth. She has never felt that her name truly belonged to her before, until his voice made her as beautiful as a rose.

He'll come soon. If she holds her breath till it hurts. Count to a hundred. *I'm coming*. She clenches her fists, breathes in a deep breath and holds it until the darkness fizzes. But when she opens her eyes it's the same blackout. The rain splashes. If he doesn't come, if he can't come, if he's tried to get a message to her –

Or if he's somewhere else. Someplace else, he'd say. Stepping into step with someone else, someone else's body going soft and shivery against his.

'What'd you say your name was?'

'Frederick. Frederick Lafayette.'

'That's a funny name.'

'It ain't funny where I come from, ma'am.'

And the milky smile shows, like a baby's. And the way he calls a girl ma'am when he doesn't know her name. Maybe he already knows that people like to hear words they would never put in their own mouths, maybe he already knows how the sweet formality of it marries with that smile. At first she thought he was one of those men who mean nothing by their talk. Later she understood that he was reserved, like her, but living in a crowd had taught him ways of getting along without getting close.

'Hey, how you doing?'

Is he doing all of that with someone else? Lucky it's dark so no one can see her face. Nobody's ever going to guess how much she wants him. She's had him now, hundreds and hundreds and hundreds of time, in parks and bus shelters and in her mind. Most of all in her mind. Out of all those hundreds, only a dozen or so in flesh and blood. He's in her mind, he won't go out of it. And deep down below all the doubts she knows she's got him too, at least for now. He can't help it any more than she can. She knows it when his voice flukes up and he sounds as if he's in pain. 'What you doing to me, Rose? You tell me what you call this.'

She doesn't know what she calls it. She's caught in it, like a cat dancing in a rainstorm that's forgotten its own nature so far it doesn't even remember to hate the wet. She, Rose, who never put a paw out of place before. At all the wrong times she imagines herself naked, with him. It wouldn't surprise her to find herself lit up at night, as if someone had painted her skin with the stuff that makes clock fingers glow in the dark. In the typing pool, the clatter of keys and the jingle of the carriage return fades, and she's with Frederick, peeling off her stockings, tangling her legs in his. But the smell of women brings her back to the big room where they sit in rows, in uniform, beating out words.

At the end of basic training last year, she saw her own reflection in the eyes of the officer who was checking length of hair and absence of jewellery. Her own body, packed away in a rating's uniform for the duration. She blinked and shifted her gaze from the regulation eyes front. She was part of a row of women standing at attention, quiveringly still. But inside she was prickling with life, her skin burning, her hair springing under her cap. The uniform didn't do away with that, it made it stronger.

Basic training was a shock to some of the girls. It wasn't so much getting up at dawn and being yelled out and working all the hours God sent and then being told to do it again, but the fact that nothing was personal. It didn't bother Rose. They thought they were knocking you into shape, but what they didn't reckon on were all the things that had shaped you already, and knocked you till you all but went down and stayed down. But you didn't, and you never would.

Rose looked light but she was tireless. She wasn't afraid to heave coal, riddle the huge boilers, shovel out the clinker, and wash down the boiler-room walls.

The only thing she didn't like was scrubbing corridors. It was the way they wanted you down on your hands and knees, arse in the air, skin chapped to the elbows. There were mops but they wanted scrubbing-brushes used in basic training. And maybe for ever after: that was the way the Navy was. But it wouldn't be Rose doing the scrubbing, not after these two weeks.

Rose's mother had scrubbed like a demon in her bad

spells. Floors, walls, windows, chairs, table. On those days Rose had come home from school and smelled the carbolic and her heart had sunk. The little ones were out in the yard. They were wary, quiet as mice, sheltering by the coal bunker and waiting for Rose. As soon as they saw her they rushed to grab her round the waist. They wanted their dinner, they hadn't had their dinner. Rain clung to their clothes but they hadn't dared ask to go in. Dickie and Iris were scared of Mum when she got her bad times, not that she would ever lay a finger on them but that she became a stranger and looked through them.

Rose knew as soon as she smelled carbolic that there'd be no more school for days, maybe weeks, depending how Mum was. She couldn't be left when she was bad. She would clean until her hands bled and then all the life would die out of her and she'd lie on her bed eating nothing, drinking a cup of tea if Rose was lucky, speaking to no one. When Dad came back from work he would look into the bedroom, and go out again without eating the tea Rose had made. Rose couldn't blame him. She'd have done the same herself if it wasn't for Dickie and Iris.

Rose never let them see that she hated scrubbing the floors. She wouldn't give them that satisfaction. She did what she had to do, never spoke to an officer unless spoken to, rolled up her hair so it didn't touch her collar, kept her place where she belonged. A part of her stood separate. Nothing would get the better of her. After basic training she was going to train as a typist. If she got on, she might become a telephonist one day, or even a radio operator. With the war, there were chances there'd never been before. She'd have something for life, that no one could take away when the war was over. That was the reason she'd volunteered for the Wrens, or part of it. She wasn't going to wait to be called up. They might send her anywhere. She'd end up in a factory, making shells to the din of *Workers' Playtime*, or shovelling swill on a farm in the back end of nowhere, under a sky the colour of mud, while some pig-ignorant farmer tried to get her into his bed.

Uniform's all right, it saves coupons. If she'd been able to go to the grammar school she'd have worn uniform there. A black blazer with a gold crest on the left pocket. She thinks the thought quickly then sheers off from it. She's in uniform now, like everyone else. But when Frederick walks towards her, all fine and supple with life, she can't turn aside from the thought of the death he's kitted out for.

Thick rain continues to fall. It's April, a sharp night but not cold. There's a cough in the dark close to her, and Rose shivers. There'll be couples all along the row of bus shelters, locked together the way she wants to be. In the dark each pair carves out its tiny privacy and the rain on the roof drowns out the sounds they make. Rose tenses, listening, feeling her uniform skirt rasp her knee through the nylons Frederick has given her. She must be mad, wasting nylons on uniform. It'd be against regulations if anyone thought a girl would be stupid enough to do it. Probably is against regulations.

5

The dark blue uniform suits Rose. She has the kind of body that makes itself felt through boxy cloth. And then there's Rose's skin, that fine-grained olive skin that looks good when fair-skinned girls flag from lack of sleep. Rose neither flags nor blooms.

'Where're you from?' Frederick Lafayette asked her the first time she danced with him.

'Staffordshire,' she said. 'The Black Country.'

He laughed, deep in his chest then high and sweet like a little boy. As soon as she heard it she wanted to make him laugh again. That voice of his. That grain in his liquid voice, like comb suspended in a honey-jar.

'How come you call it that?' he said. She soon found that he had two ways of speaking, as she had. His home voice, and then something flatter, for everyday and officers. It took a minute for him to feel his way back inside his real voice, each time he was with her. And Rose dropped the voice she'd been learning so that one day, if the war went on long enough, she could be a telephonist, a wireless operator . . .

'It's a real place,' she said. 'Do you know where the Midlands are?' Probably he thought all Brits were the same, living elbow to elbow on their packed, rainy little island. The Yanks didn't seem to think life over here had any scale. One she'd met didn't know there were other cities beside London. He'd laughed disbelievingly when she told him about Manchester and Birmingham, as if they were villages she was trying to make big.

But Frederick frowned. 'They give us a map,' he said coolly. He was a reader. An electrician by trade, but he went to night school back home, to study Economics.

He intended to go to college one day, when the war was over. He reckoned that there'd be scholarships for GIs.

'How about you? Were you a college girl?' he asked the second time they met. She glanced sharply at him, but he was serious. He couldn't tell about British accents, any more than she could tell about American ones. He really believed she might be a college girl. College over there meant university here, she knew that. His mistake struck inside her like a bell, shaking everything.

'I got a scholarship to the grammar school,' she told him. 'But I had to get a job.'

He nodded. She saw that he understood. He knew that things were the way they were.

'I went to look at the grammar school once,' she went on, telling him something she'd never told anyone. 'It was over the other side of town, so I went on the bus after work. It was getting dark and they'd locked the gates. I looked through the railings. There were still some lights on in the buildings. They were huge, those buildings. Like another town inside the town, separate.'

He said nothing. Did not bring out any experience of his own, did not say she'd done well for herself since. He put out his hand and cupped the side of her face. It was the softest touch she had ever felt. His fingers touching her jawline as if it was beautiful. She rested her head in his cupped palm.

Everyone is in uniform. You learn to look for the body inside drab greys and blues and khakis. People are hidden, even from themselves, for the duration. But it doesn't stop them finding each other. It's like a game, Rose thinks, the biggest game of blind-man's buff there's ever been. Everyone sent away from home and friends and family, turned around and around until they're dizzy, then sent off with their arms outstretched and their eyes covered, to find whoever's hiding.

A couple of yards from Rose the red tip of a cigarette pricks the dark. It lights up a man lounging against the back wall of the bus shelter, his hands cupped, looking down. Then the soft, pitchy curtain of rain and blackout settles round her again. The man must have turned aside, because she can't see his cigarette end any more. But he hasn't moved away. She'd have heard him. She's an expert on footfalls, man or woman, boot or shoe.

She can hear trains clunking in the yard. Always trains now, night and day. Things are hotting up. Everyone knows it's coming. A vast prickling excitement is building over the tiredness they won't get rid of ever, not if they sleep for a month of Sundays. Ask any one of the girls what she wants most and she'll say, 'To have my sleep out.'

He'll go soon. That's what he's over here for, to go. All those tall easy Yanks, full of food from the PX. Food Rose hadn't seen in years until she met Frederick. Tinned ham and corned beef and tinned pineapple. It's true that eating as much meat as you want gives you a different energy. The Yanks are full of it. They spill out of their lit-up cities and come over here not really believing in the darkness. Next to them, the British look thin and tired. But the same thing's coming to all of them. Tension's like a boil, swollen to bursting-point. Fights break out and are broken up. Trains clank down the rails all day and all night. It's coming. Everybody knows it and they speak about it in a different voice from the voice that's served for long grey years. Something's coming that you want and want but when it's so close you can nearly touch it you're afraid too. You want to pull back, to hide in waiting again.

It's always when she stops thinking of him coming that he comes. A finger touches the top of her spine. His voice grazes her ear.

'Jeezus, I didn't have a hope in hell I'd still find you here. You wet, baby? You got rain on those pretty shoes?'

They laugh. He has small feet for a tall man and Rose's feet in their uniform boats look nearly as big as his.

'Don't start on my feet again,' says Rose.

'I have no *intention* of starting there,' he assures her gravely. 'Come on. We're gonna go find us a park.'

It's easy in the dark. No one sees them. They're a court-ing couple like any other, hungry for their own patch of earth that's stayed dry under the canopy of laurel. There's an etiquette to finding your space. You can be three yards from another couple, but you don't see them and they don't see you. At night everyone is free, even Rose and Frederick. The park is safe, not like the street. When they walk down the streets, Rose watches ahead, bracing herself when she sees a clump of men in uniform. The ratings are rowdy, but some of the GIs scare her. The white ones. They spit on the ground as she passes with Frederick. They look at Frederick with something she hasn't ever seen on any man's face before when he looks at another man. Not before a fight, not anywhere.

'They bring their Jim Crow law over here with them,' Frederick says. The Americans separate their army into two armies, black and white. That's Jim Crow law, Frederick says. She tells him of a story she's heard, about an old farmer way down in Devon somewhere. They asked him what he thought of the Yanks stationed nearby. 'I love the Americans but I don't like those white ones they've brought along with them,' he said. Frederick told her how his daddy had brought the family from Atlanta, Georgia up north to Chicago, and never gone back. Never would go back, never would set a foot south of the line again. Not for a visit, not for nothing. His daddy was buried in Chicago soil. He'd never wanted that Atlanta earth to touch his body again.

Those white GIs would scare her if she let them. They see her walking with Frederick and you would think it was their country, not hers. Once, in the crush of the pavements, a GI grabbed her breast. Openly, although Frederick held her arm. As if Frederick wasn't a man. He grabbed and kneaded, tweaking her nipple, grinning at his mates to show them, as if she was anybody's. Frederick was looking ahead the way he did, his face impassive. In the crowd, he didn't see what happened. Rose said nothing. There were too many of them, too close. She hardened herself too, shutting her nostrils from the close, angry smell of them and from the beer on their breath. She shut her ears to the things they said. She stared straight ahead, as Frederick did and would not give them the satisfaction of knowing that she felt anything.

They'd be gone soon, she told herself, and she felt easier. But then she remembered that when they went, so would Frederick.

The park is full of scents. There's the sharp smell of city earth, and a honeyish smell from a shrub she can't name. Rain rolls off the leaves and spatters their clothes and skin as they push through the branches. Rose doesn't like the park, but it's the only place. They find a space and he spreads his jacket on the earth. It's damp, but she's known worse. When they first met it was January, with slush on the ground, a raw wind fingering up her skirt and Frederick with the worst head cold he'd had in his entire life.

They lie under the dirty old laurels, on the dirty old ground. 'Welcome to the black country,' he says. It's an old joke between them now. She tells him that one day she'll take him to see the real thing. What would Iris and Dickie make of Frederick? Iris is bashful. She won't say much to anyone she doesn't know. But Dickie's gone the other way, living his own life at thirteen, hardly coming home except to sleep. She doesn't have to worry about what Mum and Dad think. Mum's been dead five years now, and Dad's married again. Iris is still living with them, but she wants to lodge above the shop where she works. She told Rose about it, secretly, last time Rose was there.

'But Auntie Vi doesn't want me to leave home.'

'She's no more your auntie than my elbow. And it's your wages she doesn't want to leave home,' Rose pointed out.

'She's all right, Rose.'

'She's soft. She'll do anything he tells her.'

'I'll wait until I'm sixteen, then I'll go.'

'You're only fourteen and a half.'

'I know.' Iris ducked her head so her hair slipped forward over her cheeks.

'Listen, Iris. Soon as I get a place of my own, after this war's over, you can come to me. And Dickie too if he wants.'

Iris looked up. Disbelief and longing fought in her face, but the idea was too big for her. 'It's a nice room, Rose. It's lovely. Mrs Lambert let me go up and look at it. It's got a window that looks over the street. You can sit and look down on the people. All their hats go bobbing underneath you and they never look up so they never know you're there. 'F you open the window a crack you can hear what they're saying. I was thinking, I could sit there after work. And Mrs Lambert's going to let me paint the walls.'

'Where're you going to get paint from?'

'I know, but when you can. After the war.'

'She'll let you hook your own rag rug as well, will she?' asked Rose sarcastically. But Iris just gave the willing smile she used to hide the times when she wasn't following.

'It was nice the way Mum gave us both flower names,' she said at last. Iris was always busy like that, cobbling up a mum for herself out of nothing. A mum who thought about her and loved her but just happened to have gone away.

'Maybe she knew he was going to marry a woman called Violet, after she was dead.'

Iris rose silently and went out. Rose lit a cigarette and dragged in smoke. She wanted to smash everything in the room. After a while she stood up and went into the back kitchen. Iris lifted her face from the blue-and-white towel that had hung from a wooden bar as long as Rose could remember, washed so often that the blue had all but gone. That towel's lasted longer than my mother, Rose thought suddenly, remembering her mother's hands fastening it back in place after the wash.

She must not say such things to Iris. Iris's face was mottled with crying. Those red patches always sprang up on the same place, on her temples and around her eyes. When she was a kid it took hours to calm Iris down after one of her do's.

'Here, have a drag of a fag,' said Rose, handing the cigarette to Iris.

A faint smile appeared. Iris took the cigarette with a practised gesture.

'You are a daft ha'porth,' Rose said.

'I know.'

'I brought chocolate for you too.'

'Chocolate!'

'American chocolate. It's called a Hershey Bar.'

'Where'd you get it, Rose?'

'That's for you to ask, and me to know. Here, catch.'

'Are you courting a Yank, Rose?'

'Maybe.'

'What's he like?'

'Handsome.'

'Did he give you those nylons too?'

'No, that was the man in the moon.'

'Can I try them on?'

'You're taller than me. Your suspenders'll burst them.'

Iris was tall, like Dad. She looked beggingly at Rose, her mouth full of chocolate.

'Please, Rose! Just so's as I can see how they look on me.'

Her sister's legs were long and pale. The stockings only went halfway up her thighs. American Tan stretched over white skin. That's what some girls call soldiers like Frederick. Tan GIs.

Rose and Frederick know just how many buttons to undo, how far to pull up her skirt. Rose arches her back automatically to unfasten the hooks of her brassiere. Then she looks around. The rain has stopped and the sky is clearing fast. A thick, curdy mass of cloud blows over a brighter space where the moon is hidden. They are the only ones left under the laurels now. She thinks that the other couples must have gone because of the rain, dripping and seeping everywhere. But it's not as dark as it was. Now she can see him a little. Quickly, Rose pushes his hands aside and kneels up.

'Rose, what you doing?' he complains.

'Wait.'

She sheds clothes. Skirt, jacket, blouse, petticoat, brassiere, suspenders, stockings, knickers. They peel off and fall away like cards in the hands of a dealer. Rose piles them out of the way, quick and neat as always. She kneels up, naked. Can he see her?

He can. 'Jeez, Rose, look at you.'

'You do it too.'

'What if somebody comes? You want to get me court-martialled?'

'Yes.'

He hesitates, on the brink of the cold water where she is already far out. And then he smiles. She hears the smile in his voice, though there's not enough moonlight to see it by.

'OK,' he says slowly, 'OK. If that's the way you want it.'

He takes off his clothes more slowly than her, folding each item with a care that shows her he is suddenly nervous as he's never been before. Then he's naked, too. She puts out her hand and it shows pale against his arm. She has never seen him like this before. She does not really know what he looks like. They know each other by touch, through clothes, standing up on the coldest of nights, lying down where they can.

Rose lies on top of him for a long while. Neither moves. If one of them moves an inch it will all start, a ripple in one flesh spreading to the other. How long can they hold still, like this? She can't tell where he ends and she begins. He's different from the other men she's known, who have no sooner got her legs open than they are pumping into her as if there's a fire, their faces twisted and their weight crushing her breath. Afterwards they don't want to talk, don't really want to see her even. They haul themselves off her with a suck and a heave. They have no idea that there's anything left to want. Worst of all are the ones who are doggily grateful, as if it's all been done for their sake, a gift they got away with because Rose is stupid, or easy. And maybe most of the time that's true, thinks Rose.

Suddenly she is chilled, and as lonely inside herself as she's been all those other times. She moves one leg, very slightly, against his thigh. She skims her right hand across his chest and touches his nipple, the feathery touch she's learned from him. He gasps deep in his throat, between a laugh and a groan. She leans forward. His face snaps sideways and he begins to move inside her. She tastes his mouth as if it is a fruit she's read about but never imagined she would eat.

It is cold now. The moon's brighter, too bright. Rose can hear wind tickling the leaves along the path. It sounds like the rustling of a newspaper with bad news in it. As soon as they've done it, outside comes pressing in on them, she thinks. Their heads, screened by rhododendrons, are only a few feet from the path. Twice she's heard footsteps. She moves her head so that she can see past Frederick's shoulder, and looks up at the moon through the laurel leaves. It's still pushing back the night clouds. For a second she lets her gaze follow the long curve of his shoulder, his back, hip, buttock, thigh, then the legs going away. She can't see his feet at this angle.

But if she can see him, so can anyone. Military police patrol this park with torches sometimes. Frederick eases himself up on his elbows, and looks down at her. She wonders what he can see, but for once she can't find her mirror face to look back with. She just lies there and lets him see her, naked as a baby. Then he is up and brushing loose dirt from his hands, bending over his pile of clothes. Rose sees that he is ready to turn from her, back into the world of uniforms.

'If my mama could see me now,' he says, looking down at Rose over his shoulder.

Rose does not reply. She does not want to hear about anyone's mama. She knows enough about Frederick's family. His brother who is still in junior high. His baby sister, and his father in the Chicago soil. Every time he speaks of them she hears responsibility in his voice. He has got to take care of them. His brother is a bright kid and he'll have the chances that time wasn't right for Frederick to have.

His voice is telling her that his life is elsewhere, not here in these rainy parks he soon won't see again. Better his family don't come too close, get too real. Would they like her? What would they think about Frederick going with a white girl? A Brit, that's what they'd call her. She'd be foreign to them. The brother is going to college one day. *If my brother don't study hard my mama will whup his ass and then I'll come home and whup it a second time.* Frederick smiles as he says it. Rose guesses that there won't be too much whupping required. Frederick has confidence in a brother who doesn't need to be driven, in a future that's burning its way out of the past. What would his family say to Iris, and Dad, and Auntie Vi?

Elsewhere is nowhere, Rose thinks. These days are what we've got. You have to take what you can.

Quickly they get dressed like strangers, back to back. But at the last moment, late as they are, he wraps his arms around her again. Soon he is rocking her and they are cheek to cheek.

'Cold,' he says. 'I ain't been warm since I left home.'

She tries to remember where Chicago is on the map.

'Is it warm in winter, where you come from?'

He laughs. 'Uh-uh. But it's a different style of cold back home. I never been bone-chilled like here. We better go now, Rose.'

'I want to live near the sea,' she says abruptly. 'The noise of it.' Another thing she has never told anyone.

'That's why you joined the Wrens?'

She laughs. 'No, it was because of the buttons.'

'The buttons?'

'Yeah. Wrens don't have brass buttons. If you have buttons, you have to polish them and they have to shine all the time.'

'You worked that one out before you joined up?'

She nods, feeling her head move in the hollow of his shoulder. But then her voice comes again, muffled.

'It was the sea. I'd never seen the sea.'

When you are slack with love you get careless. Rose and Frederick step out of the park, but nothing outside their two bodies touches them. By the rank overgrowth of privet at the park gates she hears rustling, snuffling, and thinks of badgers though there are no badgers here. The gates are shut but with the railings gone it's easy to climb over the stone wall studded with stumps of metal. She goes first, with Frederick holding her hand to steady her, and then he follows. Down onto the pavement under the street lamp with its muffled blackout glow. But they're all right because they know where they are going. This is their place.

'Nigger lover,' says a voice by her ear. She's so far from herself that for a second she thinks it's a joke. It's a Yank voice, like Frederick's.

'Fuckin nigger lover,' says a second voice, and then another. They are coming at her from everywhere. Then shadows pull away from the dark. Three men, four, five. They don't wait, don't say any more, don't shape up for a fight. Just fall on Frederick, banging Rose to one side so she slams into the stone wall.

She grates against the rough stone as she falls. She is down on the ground. She touches the side of her face where it hurts and her fingers come away slimy with blood. But Frederick is gone. She wants to call to him but cunning sits on her tongue, holding it down. They mustn't know that she can move.

She looks down the wet pavement into where it's happening. There is a mess of dark, jostling shapes, down on the ground. They've got him down. She knows that in a fight you mustn't fall. You have got to stay on your feet. She heard Dad teach Dickie that. If they get a boot to your head you won't get up again. She clambers painfully on to all fours, pushes herself off the wall, begins to stagger towards them. But one of them turns casually, sees her coming, and throws her off easily as if she's nothing. The back of her head hits the pavement.

She lies there looking up. There is a taste of vomit in her mouth. Maybe she has been sick without remembering it. Her ears are noisy, as if they've got water in them. The moon is still up there. It is looking at her more brightly than she could ever look at it. She can't remember why she is down here looking at the moon, and then she can. She raises her head but it won't hold up, she raises it again and heaves herself over and begins to crawl forward with her head down. But they are too far and she can't get to them. The fight is moving down the pavement away from her, taking Frederick with it. There are terrible noises coming out of it that don't sound like anyone she has ever known. She is crying out now, trying to reach the bodies that sway and lunge. They have got him on the ground she knows it and she can hear him grunting groaning as if they are on top of him and his life is being pushed out of him like the little ones being pushed out of Mum while Rose sat in the yard and played with pebbles.

'Frederick!' she screams, but he doesn't answer and what happens is that one of them leaves the pack and falls on her. He drags her up off the ground, he gets hold of her head, he is grappling for her mouth but his fingers miss and poke her right eye. She screams again. He is blinding her but she knows no one will come. She can smell the man, his sweat and something he puts on his hair and his uniform smell and his PX food smell. Some parts of his smell are the same as Frederick but most of it is strangeness. He pulls her head back and gets his whole right hand over her mouth, half over her nose too so that she struggles for breath, lashing out with feet and nails. She twists her head, trying to get a grip, trying to bite his hand. His left hand grips her throat.

'You carry on like that, I'm gonna hurt you.'

Her eyes are bursting in her head, hurting her. She can't see the moon. All she hears are her own whimpers.

They are gone. She's down on the pavement and she needs to stay there. Her cheek is against the stone and the cold stone is greasy with rain. She lifts her head and looks in terror along the length of the ground, trying to focus.

He is there. She knows it's him though the shape on the ground looks smaller than Frederick, even when he's lying down. She shuffles towards him on her knees, saying his name. The moon is weak now. She can see him but not yet name the parts of him. Slowly the shape thrust towards her becomes the sole of his boot. She raises herself on her elbows to see him.

He is on his back, arms cast up around his head. He looks as if he's been thrown there. His face is sideways, his eyes almost shut but not quite. A strip of white shows. She shuffles until her face is touching his, and feels for his breath with her fingers.

It's there. She can feel it. She thinks she can feel it. But his face is split, pulped like a fruit.

'Frederick? Frederick!'

But he doesn't answer. His lips are open. His top front teeth are gone.

She looks down the long, shining pavement. At the far end, a hundred yards away, a shadowy couple walk, twined together. They are in a world of their own. They saw nothing, heard nothing. She begins to call and wave her arms as if she and Frederick are far out to sea, clinging to the hull of an upturned boat. The couple drifts on, out of sight.

'What'd they do to you?' he asks her. His voice is grating. That's because his windpipe was hurt where they tried to throttle him. He clears his throat as if he's got a cold.

'Nothing,' she says quickly. 'They held me down, that's all.'

Suddenly she realises what he's been afraid of. He thinks they raped her, to show her that she's anyone's. That's why he hasn't wanted to see her all these days. That's why the nurses were told to say he was too sick to see anyone. The swellings are down and the stitches due to come out. He has had an operation on his jaw, which is broken in three places. They've put a plate in.

'You reckon they'll be giving me a medal?' says Frederick. His voice is a thousand miles away from her. The gap in his teeth makes his words seem to stumble.

'They didn't touch me,' she says urgently. But he just nods, neither believing nor disbelieving. She puts her hand on his arm and he lets it lie there. His face has changed so much, as if they've tried to put everything back right but did not know where the right places were. She could have told them. Now she sees that the smallest change to a face makes it so that you can't read it any more. Eyes, forehead, cheeks, mouth. She looks at them. His skin colour is different, ashy with what pain's done to him. Deep bruising still discolours his face around the jawline. They stove in three ribs, she knows that. The nurse told her. His collarbone was dislocated, but they fixed that. There are other troubles. A catheter line leads from the bed to a glass jar. Rose is afraid to ask Frederick about his injuries. She would have asked a nurse, but they are all in a hurry, clacking past as if the visitors are trouble they don't want.

'My mama wrote me,' Frederick says abruptly, nodding towards his locker. This is the face that lay so close to hers that they seemed to share the same breath. The locker top is smooth and empty. He must have put the letter away. He didn't want anyone to see it.

'She don't know nothin bout all this and she ain't ever gonna know nothin,' he continues.

'What's her name?' says Rose at last.

'Lucile.'

'That's a nice name.'

'Yeah. Pretty. She writes she's prayin for me night and day, cause she knows I'll be goin into danger soon. Mama's a Baptist. Not my daddy though, he was political.'

He is talking in the voice he must have had as a child. His eyes are turned away from her. He is back with them, not with her.

'He brought us out of Georgia when I was eight months old,' he goes on. 'My daddy used to tell us stories. They weren't fit for a child's ears, my mama said, but he said we should know them. That way we would understand what the law was for, and why you have to get to a place that has laws the same for everyone. He used to say that we hadn't reached that place yet and maybe we never would reach it. But we were on our way. Cause it ain't right for people to do what they like. I used to wonder when my daddy said that. Used to think it'd be pretty good to do just what I liked.'

She is tiring him. She takes his hand, but it lies slack in hers. She releases it gently, to rest on the boiled bedcover, palm up.

'Frederick,' she says. His gaze slides towards her, and then away. The whites of his eyes are still bloodshot and yellow.

'I never was baptised,' he says. 'I never heard that call. I followed my daddy.'

There is a film of sweat on his forehead now. Soon the nurse will come and tell her that he needs to rest. Those doctors and nurses think they know everything. Dad wouldn't let a doctor near Mum, because they'd have taken her away. Better she lay there, her toes poking up under the bedclothes and her face shut. She lay like that for weeks sometimes, and the bad times came more and more often until the good times were squeezed to nothing between them.

That nurse is crackling her way down the ward towards them. twitching bedcovers and checking charts. Visiting hour is over.

'Goodbye, Rose,' he says.

What's left? There's nothing left.

'I'll come again tomorrow,' she says. She'll come and come and each time he will be there, not here. She wants to seize him back, all of him, pull him back across the ocean from where he's gone. She knows where

Chicago is now. She's looked at the map. Chicago lies on a lake as big as the sea, but it's hemmed in by thousands of miles of land. The lake is so big that they even have tides there, it says so in the back of the atlas. But they are not real tides. You'd think from the size of the lake that it was the sea, and that you could sail away on it to anywhere in the world. But you never could.

Whales and Seals

Shannon cuts the boat's engine, and here we are, drifting on the Pacific Ocean. Without the noise of the engine it's clear how fragile we are, just a speck of metal and flesh in a wilderness of water. But the thought doesn't trouble me.

'We're in US territorial waters now,' says Shannon.

She's a tawny-skinned New Zealander with a beautiful smile and a passion for marine biology. The amount she's told us already would fill a guidebook, and I haven't listened to all of it. But I've kept a listening look on my face, because I like Shannon. She's working her way around the world, and then she'll do her Ph.D. on Baltic herring.

'Baltic herring, Shannon?'

'Yeah, crazy, isn't it? Maybe it's because my father's Estonian.'

Shannon gets up from her seat and beams at the rest of her passengers.

'We're in US waters now, guys! Got your passports handy?'

The man in front of me lifts his camcorder and begins to film the flat silvery US ocean.

'You can go out on deck if you like,' says Shannon.

Deck is tiny. If we're polite and not pushy there's room for the ten of us, and because of the big silence lapping round us it doesn't feel crowded. Everyone's mind is away out there on the ocean. We've seen sea lions, and cormorants, and a school of Dall's porpoises that rushed the boat. I was afraid of the boat injuring them, but Shannon said it wouldn't happen. 'They like to ride the bow wave,' she said. 'They like the feeling of it. Sometimes they'll get onto the bow wave of one of those big freighters and ride it for hours. Maybe it conserves energy. Maybe they're just playing.'

We haven't seen whales yet. I look across the water at the Olympus mountain range. The mountains are snow-covered, and a breath of chill comes off the Pacific water. It's too cold for us to swim here. But the whales like it. The water is cold and rich, packed with chains of life that man hasn't broken. Not here, not yet. Shannon tells us that an orca can eat four hundred pounds of salmon in a day. The only way I can imagine that quantity of salmon is to build a tower of supermarket steaks in my mind. Three hundred, maybe? I used to buy four salmon steaks and they would weigh maybe a pound and a half. One for Luke, one for Jasmine, one for Don, one for me. I would ask the assistant to make sure the steaks were the same size. If one steak was bigger than the others I would cover it with sauce to hide the fact.

Maybe we aren't going to see any whales, not today. The man with the camcorder is asking Shannon if she thinks they'll come.

'Yes,' says Shannon. 'They're around. They were here this morning. This time of the day, they're feeding. I'll have a listen.'

She goes to the back of the boat and fiddles with the

underwater acoustic device which she's already explained to us.

'Listen,' she says. All of us fall silent and listen obediently to noises which sound like music you'd turn off on Radio 3.

'They're hunting salmon. Hear that clicking? There's one quite close. Fifty metres off, maybe.'

We're all staring out at the bald silver sea, willing it to yield up a whale. I hold my breath. The boat twirls slowly on a current I can't see. Land is far off. Please, I say inside myself. *Please.* Our boat bobs like a little ark of prayer. All of us holding our breath, all of us wanting and waiting. Do the whales come at all? Is this whole trip a gigantic pretend, like putting your baby tooth in a glass of water by your bed so the tooth fairy can replace it with a coin, or staying awake on Christmas Eve to catch a glimpse of Father Christmas, even though you know he's really your dad? I've been the fairy myself too many times. I've filled those stockings. Why am I holding my breath like a child?

Shannon scours the waters with her binoculars. I turn away. I'm not going to look any more. I'm not going to let those whales know that I'm desperate.

Suddenly, casually, on the other side of the boat, the whale is there. A black curve breaks the water. Much too big for a porpoise. Sleek and streaming and then it's gone. I pull at Shannon's arm.

'There. There. Over there. It's a whale. I saw a whale.'

'Hey, you did?' She acts thrilled and surprised, and I know she's never had any doubts. Of course the whales would come.

'Hey, guys, over here,' says Shannon, lifting her voice, and everyone stares at the water where the whale was. And then the water is live with whales. A back shows above the water again, a fin rises, a tail lifts in the perfect forked whale shape we all know from a thousand pictures.

'There's two of them.'

'Over there. Look. It's another. It dived, just there.'

No one calls out or rushes to the side. Calm spreads over the boat and the water as the whales show themselves more and more. They are playing, I'm sure of it, not hunting. They are playing with us. I stare, trying to print it on my mind for ever. Whales in the grey, shining Pacific which turns dark in the distance. Their clicking sounds bubble through the acoustic device.

'There's Shaker,' says Shannon.

'Shaker?'

'Yeah, it's him, his mum'll be around here too.'

'Do you give them all names?'

I'm not sure I like the idea of this. They aren't pets. They're *whales*.

'Yeah, pretty much. Shaker's really playful.'

'Is he a baby whale?' I ask foolishly.

'Nah, he's twenty-five, twenty-six. But these whales stay with their mothers all their lives. He's got a sister in this pod too. If his mum dies he'll stay with her.'

'All their lives – really?'

'If you think of it, it makes sense,' says Shannon. 'Their home is the pod. They won't leave unless there's something seriously wrong.'

'Like what?'

'There was a big story last year about a whale that got separated from the pod. Boats were tracking it, people were wanting to reunite it. But it wasn't lost. It had something wrong, some genetic issue, and the pod rejected it. That can happen.'

'Oh.'

'That's tough,' says a young woman in a red jacket.

'No sentiment in the animal kingdom,' says the man with the camcorder.

'I don't know,' says Shannon surprisingly. 'Whales have deep feelings, I do know that.'

She lifts her binoculars again, and is silent. She's a sensitive girl. She wants this to be our experience, not hers.

The whale she called Shaker has disappeared. There are two more whales moving through the water in the distance, west to east, sometimes showing, sometimes not. They travel purposefully. Even though I can see them clearly, it doesn't make them any less mysterious.

Everyone in the boat is filming or taking photos. I take some photos myself and think of showing them to Luke. But they won't come out the way it was. My photos rarely do. I'm always having to explain what's in them.

'See that shape there, Luke? No, not there, there. That's part of a whale. Which part? Um, well, maybe it's the back. Or it could be the tail –'

The young woman in the red jacket taps my arm. 'You want me to take a photo of you with a whale in the background?'

Close up, I see how bright and eager she is. It would be churlish to turn her down.

She takes a long time, trying to get the best shot, waiting for a whale to rise behind me. At last it's done.

'He was distant, but it should come out OK.'

'Thanks a lot. Do you want me to take one of you?'

She hands me her camera. 'It'll be something to show my kids. They're back at the hotel. They're so jealous of me for taking this trip, but three and five, they're pretty young for it. And it's expensive –'

'You have every right to take a trip on your own,' I say firmly. 'That's what I'm doing, too.'

'You got kids?'

'Two.'

'I'm Julie, I'm from Moose Jaw. Yeah, I know. You're British, right? It's a real place, that's what it's called. I was born there.'

By the time we've all finished taking photos, a wind off the mountains is chopping up the water. The whales have hidden themselves. It's time to go back.

We settle ourselves in the cramped cabin. Shannon starts the engine and our boat bucks and slaps across the water. The engine noise makes me sleepy, but Shannon is telling us something above the racket.

'We'll be going by a seal colony on the way back. I'll cut the engine and take you as close as I can, but we don't want to scare them off the rocks.'

She tells us about seals. How the transient killer whales work in groups to scare seals off the rocks and wait for them on the other side once they hit the water. How the seal pups are independent at six weeks.

'Six weeks!' says Julie. 'Seal moms sure get a better

deal than whale moms. Didn't you say that Shaker was still hanging out with his mother at twenty-three?'

'He'll still be hanging out with her at forty, if she's alive,' says Shannon.

'Oh my Lord. Forty years. Can you picture that?'

My answering smile is as quick as I can make it.

When Luke is forty I shall be sixty-six. Still able to take care of him, unless something happens. Luke will be forty and probably his hair will be grey. My child's hair will be grey.

'How old are your kids?' asks Julie.

'Jasmine is nineteen, Luke is twenty-three.'

'They've flown the nest, then.' Like most parents of small children, she still sees their upbringing as a finite task. They will get to the sunlit uplands of adulthood at eighteen and that will be it. Job done.

'Jasmine's at uni. Luke is at home with us.'

And as her expression changes slightly I decide to tell her.

'He was in an accident last year. A car accident. He wasn't driving. He had head injuries.'

'I'm so sorry,' says Julie. 'How is he doing?'

'Better than we thought. Much better than we thought. But he won't be able to manage on his own. Not for a while.'

Luke's face rises in my mind. He is wearing the strange, lost look that comes over him sometimes. I am afraid that this look comes when he really remembers that it wasn't always like this. Most of the time the facts of his former life are like a story to him. He went to university, he shared a flat, he studied Sports Science and Psychology and played in the university hockey team.

One day last month I found him standing by the washing machine with his cereal bowl and coffee mug.

'Mum,' he asked me. 'Do I know how to operate this article?'

I cannot get his frowning, pained look out of my head.

'It's great that you took this trip,' says Julie. For a moment her warm hand covers mine. 'You'll be able to tell Luke about the whales.'

'Yes.'

Yes, I will tell him. I will tell him about the cold, dark Pacific water, the American mountains, and the silence when our engine stopped. How fragile our boat was on the water. I'll tell Luke that I have been seven thousand miles away from him, on trains and boats and aeroplanes, and the whales were real.

Esther to Fanny

I am an orphan. I say these words aloud to myself and hear them move around the room and then disappear into the carpet. They sound like a lie, even though they are true. An orphan is small, scared and hopeful, battling bravely in an institution or bowling along a country road in a dog-cart towards a new home where she won't be wanted at first. Orphans have red hair, wide vocabularies, and a carpet-bag containing their earthly possessions. An orphan is a child with a destiny.

I know the literature. '*Orphans of the Storm: the journey to self-actualisation in literature for children.*' We don't yet teach a module with that title, but we may well do so one day. It has exactly the right ring to it. Our students like modules which demand opinions rather than extensive reading. My studies in English Literature have brought me here, to this room where words sink into the cord carpet, to this university staff flat in a concrete block full of students.

They are arriving now. Parents are unloading cars, lugging TVs up echoey staircases, checking the wiring on the communal microwave, opening and then quickly closing the bathroom doors. Soon they'll be gone and the kids will be on their own. Big, bonny, temporary orphans with credit cards.

My mother died during the summer. I practise the words

and they too disappear. When last term ended I was a woman with a mother whom I visited each weekend. Some colleagues knew why, others didn't. I had learned a new vocabulary. I would say, '*Macmillan nurse*', and on one or two faces there would shine complete understanding. On others, not a flicker.

Esther to Fanny, this is Esther to Fanny, come in.

I listen. I'm not daft enough to think there's going to be any answer. My name is Esther. My mother's name was not Fanny.

Last term I read out to my students a letter from a woman with breast cancer. This letter was addressed to a woman called Esther. The writer's name was Fanny, Fanny Burney, and in her letter she described a mastectomy performed on her, without anaesthetic, in 1811.

It isn't my period. It didn't fit into the module at all, and some of my students were annoyed at the waste of their time. But I thought it was worth reading to them, all the same.

I came across Fanny Burney's letter by chance, while I was searching yet another website for information about mastectomy. And there was Fanny Burney's portrait. Her face was composed but she looked as if something had amused her very much a few minutes earlier. I began to read her letter to Esther.

The eighteenth century is not my period, but it has always appealed to me. There is something about those small, fierce, brave people who dressed elaborately, smelled awful, gushed about feeling and worshipped Reason. Fanny Burney, for all she lived forty years into the nineteenth century, is one of them to the bone. I am glad it's not my period. I wouldn't want to add to it, deconstruct it, contextualise it, demystify it, or explain it in any way.

I didn't ask my students to analyse Fanny's letter. I read it out to them, that's all. They are too big and bouncing, healthy and beautiful. They frowned and shifted in their seats and flinched and probably felt glad that things like that only happen to really old people. Fanny Burney was fifty-nine! No wonder she got ill, what else could she expect? Beside, at fifty-nine, should you really care so much about your life any more? It is the deaths of children and young people that rate as tragedies, just as it is children who make real orphans. Fanny Burney's mastectomy, performed without anaesthesia, gave her another twenty-nine years of life. I watched my students doing the calculation, and reckoning that it was hardly worth it. Who wants to suffer in order to be old for even more years?

No, I am not doing them justice. They flinched, as I did. Unconsciously, some of the girls brought up their hands to cover their breasts, as I'd done. Fanny got through to them.

'I don't see why she agreed to have the operation. I mean, I'd rather die than go through that!' one girl said after I had finished reading. 'I mean, she wasn't young, was she,' she added, glancing at me.

Esther to Fanny. No, you weren't young. My mother wasn't young, either. She was even older than you. She was seventy-three. If she didn't receive the very best of modern medical treatment, she certainly had the nearly-best. She had a mastectomy, radiotherapy, chemotherapy.

Two years later she developed a secondary in her left lung. She had more radiotherapy, oxygen, a nebuliser, massage, physiotherapy to keep her lungs as clear as possible. They gave her baths in a jacuzzi at the hospice. She liked the jacuzzi, or at least I think she liked it. She was so polite that it was hard to tell.

My mother had everything. GP appointments, clinic appointments, a second opinion, referral for rehab, referral to pain clinic, a place in a trial, a re-referral, another X-ray, a series of blood-tests, a change of consultant, a lavender massage, a Macmillan nurse, a commode, a bell by her bed and a tube up her nose, a bed in the hospice. She was so lucky to get it, that bed in the hospice.

Esther to Fanny. You had none of that. Each doctor in your story had a name. They trembled, or grew pale, or stood aside hanging their heads at the thought of the pain they were about to give you. They colluded with you in sending your husband out for the day. They knew, as you did, that he would not be able to endure witnessing your operation. They told you the truth: '*Je ne veux pas vous tromper – Vous Souffrirez –* vous *souffrirez* beaucoup.'

Yes, they were clear about it. They were men of the eighteenth century, even though the century had turned. They told you that you would suffer a great deal. They told you that you must cry out and scream. They stammered, and could not go on, because their sensibility was as powerful as their sense of reason.

When the moment came for the operation to begin, you wanted to run out of the room. But Reason took command in your fierce, bright eighteenth-century mind, and you climbed onto the bedstead where your breast was to be amputated. There were seven men around your bed. I wonder how they smelled, and how often they washed? They were the greatest doctors of their age, but probably they didn't even wash their hands before they cut off your breast. They put a cambric handkerchief over your face, and through it you saw the glint of polished steel.

But they also cured you. They cut off your living breast and scraped you down to the bone to search out the last cancerous atoms. You screamed all the time, except when you fainted. You recovered, even though everyone concerned in your operation was left pale as ashes, in their black clothes. You saw the blood on them as you were carried back to your bed. You were about to live for another twenty-nine years.

It's a strange story to our ears, Fanny. How exquisitely you act out the hard logic of the eighteenth century, and keep your eyes open under the cambric handkerchief. It is only semi-transparent anyway, so you see most of what goes on as the men prepare to operate upon you. They could have found a thick black piece of cloth and tied it around your eyes as a blindfold, but they didn't. I have the feeling that they respected you too much.

And the emotion around that bed! Imagine if one of the doctors treating my mother had turned ashen, and wept. If he had told her the truth. '*Vous Souffrirez – vous souffrirez beaucoup.*'

Nobody said it. But you suffered, Mum. You suffered a great deal. There was a smell in the hospice which we never mentioned, although I know you smelled it as well as I did. It was the smell of death, literally: it was the smell of the cancer in the old man who shared your two-bed room. He was curtained, out of sight, but we could smell him. I had never known that such a thing would be. Sometimes I would gag, and turn it into a cough.

'It's not very nice, is it?' you whispered once, sadly, pitifully. But in a very soft whisper, so no one else would hear.

Esther to Fanny. I am glad that you screamed throughout the twenty minutes of your operation, except when you fainted. To restrain yourself might have seriously bad consequences, your doctors told you beforehand. What miracles of sense and feeling those men must have been! Knowing that you would scream, you must scream, and anticipating it by actually charging you to scream and informing you that to do otherwise might be dangerous for your health. Knowing that you would have enough to contend with, under that semitransparent cambric handkerchief, without any false shame.

My mother hated to make a fuss. She was very grateful to all the doctors and nurses. If they didn't do their jobs well, she had an answer for it. They were understaffed, run off their feet. *That nurse over there, Esther, she's got an eight-month-old baby, she's been up half the night with him cutting his molars. I don't know how she does it.*

I wanted to shake that nurse until her teeth rattled. She was late with the drugs round. My mother was waiting, waiting. There was sweat on her yellow face but she wouldn't let me ring the bell.

'For God's sake, Mum, it's what they're here for. They're supposed to be taking care of you, that means bringing your tablets when you need them.'

But my mother turned her head aside wearily. 'It doesn't do to get across them. You don't know, Esther.'

Esther to Fanny. You were utterly in those doctors' power, just as Mum was. You saw the flash of steel through your cambric handkerchief. You felt and heard that blade scraping your breastbone. You were a heroine and the doctors treated you as one.

We have moved on. We have chemo and radio and prosthesis, and scans to show the travels of those 'peccant attoms' of cancer which your doctors feared so much that they scraped you down to the bone. What can I say? I can't re-read your account without flinching. You couldn't re-read it at all.

Mum is dead and I'm an orphan. Two things that don't sound as if they can possibly be true. Mum didn't want to cause any trouble, and she didn't cause any trouble. The doctors barely noticed her really.

My students are pounding up and down the stairs with their posters, IKEA lamps, armfuls of CDs and clothes. They are flushed, healthy, on the whole averse to study but only too pleased to be back at uni with all their friends. Some of them will choose my module on Elizabeth Bishop. These days it is perfectly possible to get to the end of a degree in English Literature without venturing into the eighteenth century at all.

Esther to Fanny. At the end of your long letter you apologised to your sister. 'God bless my dearest Esther

– I fear this is all written – confusedly, but I cannot read it – and I can write no more –'

I put my hand out to touch that semi-transparent cambric handkerchief which time has laid across you. Your letter cuts like polished steel, although I am not, dear Fanny, your Esther at all.

Annina

That time when I was having Annina. The time I had Annina. No. It doesn't sound right. I can say: the time when I was having Blaise. In fact I have said it, often. It's my time, my experience, my possession. No one can contradict me about it.

Long ago in the middle of the night when everyone was sleeping and there was a frost on the ground which killed the last of my geraniums even though they'd lived through the whole of a mild winter, Annina was born.

It doesn't matter what I write, it comes out as lies. And that's very suitable for the story of Annina. Annina's taught me a new language entirely, one of lies and things you leave out. Without it, now, I wouldn't survive. It's more necessary to me than air to breathe.

Annina is my little girl. Annina is my language. I speak Annina. Even in quite ordinary conversations, I pick up scraps of Annina. Out of the fuzz of static which is what ordinary English has become for me, I catch a phrase. Annina.

> My little baby-waby
> My drop of honey
> My own, my secret one.

Quite often I hear lovers speaking a bit of Annina. It may be nauseating, but by God it's recognizable, like one of those tunes you just hear once and it happens that you've got a new dress on and the sun's shining so warmly you can smell both the cotton and your own skin.

But this isn't doing you justice, Annina. Here I am making a mystery out of you when all you ever wanted was to be a secret, and you're that for sure now, because even if I wanted to pick you up and brandish you for the world to see, you've gone. The traces you've left are only those that might be made by any sick-hearted woman whose son has grown up and gone, a woman who's always wanted a little girl, but whose little girl would need to be more a doll than a thing of flesh. THING. I never called you that. I did Blaise, of course.

'Come here, you bad thing, wait till Mummy catches you.'

None of that with Annina.

'My daughter', I called her, and 'my girl'.

Never little. Never creature. Never thing.

Annina was not quite small enough to sleep inside a walnut shell. The cracked shell of a hard-boiled egg, for sure, but that would have been unnecessary. It was easy enough to make things nice for her, and why shouldn't she have her own bed with pillow and sheets and quilt like any Christian? And she was a Christian, I made sure of that. The big drop of holy water swelling and breaking across her face. Her mouth squaring with anger. And I made the sign of the cross without bruising her forehead. I wasn't sure if I'd done it right, so I went to an old Jesuit in a church in the city centre and told him what I'd done; nothing about the size of Annina, for fear he'd write me off as a madwoman, but everything else.

Though maybe I could have told him, for he looked as if nothing in the world would surprise him. I'd done right, it seemed. But as I came out and felt Annina stir in her quilted sling under my blouse, I wondered why it had seemed to matter so much and why I'd gone running to the priest when there was Annina, warm and fragile as a new-laid egg. Already, even though she wasn't yet speaking, a bit of Annina's language had got between me and the priest, and somehow it wasn't the word of Annina I doubted. She was always as warm as any other child. I don't know why that should have surprised me, but it did, almost as if I thought she should have had a slighter heat to match her slight size. Or perhaps it was all the stories I used to read in my *Green Fairy Book* and my *Red Fairy Book*, where the fairies were cold and magical and lived under the hills.

But don't mistake me. Annina is no fairy.

Let's go back to when I had Annina, since there doesn't seem to be any more accurate way of putting it. Blaise was eight at the time. He was tall for his age and he'd just had his hair cut short and freckles were coming on his nose and his cheeks from playing out after school with his friends, now the days were growing longer and lighter. He was not my baby any more, but I didn't mind that. I have never wanted to be the sort of woman who stands back, bruised and brave, to let her young hero make his own way in life. And lets him know that she's always waiting for him back at home. Besides, for the first time since Blaise's birth, I was pregnant again. Not far along, about nine weeks. We'd always wanted more children, but since Blaise it'd been as if we were sitting by one of those rivers you know is full of fish, with juicy bait and a good line but not a single bite the whole afternoon. Not that we were that bothered. We'd enjoyed those afternoons, with the sun on us and the water spreading out and the chance of a little fish under the surface. No, we weren't bothered.

So I was looking at my future in a new way when one afternoon just before Blaise came home I bent down to see if the frost really had got the geraniums or not, and when I straightened up there was something warm and wet running down my legs. My first thought was that I'd wet myself. It was a long time since I'd been pregnant and anything seemed possible. But of course it was red and it was blood and at the same time it began to hurt, very slyly, as if it was mocking the period which would have come around that time of the month if I hadn't been pregnant.

And then there were hours of hot panic, with the doctor coming and being sorry but I'd lost the baby, and Matt coming home seeming to bring the noise and smell of the schoolchildren with him, since he'd come out of class so suddenly. Then Matt went downstairs to cook sausages just for Blaise, when he came home. Neither of us felt like anything.

There was a little prickle under the sheet. The first stir of that small heat I grew to know better than my own temperature. Annina.

There was a cord like a cotton thread, so I bit through

it. She was an inch and a half long and as fast asleep as if she was only halfway through her long journey, and she was damned if she was going to wake up somewhere dull in the middle of it. Not like Blaise, I thought. Blaise was born crying. And that was the first difference between them which occurred to me.

I wiped the blood off her with a corner of my nightgown, then I got up although I was still bleeding and found a box of fancy handkerchiefs in my top left-hand drawer. They were fine lace and the kind of useless thing you get given and then keep by you for years without using, but they did for Annina. She looked just like a handkerchief in my hand when Matt came into the room with a cup of tea.

'What are you doing out of bed?' he asked, and set down my cup of tea in a hurry and helped me back to lie down. All the time I held on to Annina in that light way you do when you've got something in your hand which might break, and I prayed that she wouldn't make a sound, though what kind of noise a baby her size might make, I couldn't imagine.

Of course I found out soon enough. That was the first bit of her language Annina taught me. A lighter, croakier sound than I'd thought. If I breathed in hard and groaned as if in my sleep, I could hide her cries with my own breathing. After a couple of months I couldn't breathe any other way when I lay down to sleep. Matt said to me once, gentle and awkward, 'I always knew you minded more than you let on. That was when you began groaning in your sleep.'

Feeding you, Annina! Well, you made it clear right from

the start that there was going to be no satisfying you on nectar and honey-dew. Cow's milk, boiled and cooled and strained, a drop at a time from an eye-dropper. But it gave you wind and you cried for two hours one night while I shifted about in bed and wheezed and moaned to cover it. So I asked a friend who'd had a baby born at seven months, just marvelling casually at how well she'd managed and how the little thing had thrived, and she told me they'd fed her on goats' milk right from the beginning, on her midwife's advice since her own milk had dried up after a week.

'Right, that's for you, Annina,' I said to myself, and I told Matt that I was going to drink goats' milk from now on, in the hope of curing an itchy rash I'd got between my fingers. How I hated that stuff! But you loved it. I could swear now that I saw the pink flush through your skin when you had your first feed of it, drop by drop, at blood-heat. I could see your right leg kicking as you swallowed it.

You didn't cry much after that. Often you'd be awake, for I'd feel you moving against me in the little pouch I made for you, hung around my neck and hidden by a loose blouse. Poor Matt missed the way we used to sleep together naked, skin to skin, and make love when we were half awake and half sleeping. I think he believed I'd lost heart for making love now I'd lost the baby, even though he must have known that for me that had never been the point of it. So I made a nest for you under my bed and I would tuck you there until I was sure from Matt's breathing that he was asleep. Then I'd bring you into the bed with me, because otherwise I was afraid you'd cry in the night and I wouldn't hear you. And I was afraid of other things for you: wasps and mice and spiders which would be half the size of you or more. When I started to think of dogs and cats I had to close my mind and tell myself: *Take one step at a time.*

We had no cat or dog ourselves, only a pair of goldfish which were like dolphins in your eyes. Do you remember how I let you swim in the tank with them when you begged me to let you, and the big goldfish hung quite still in the water with terror before he dived into the weed and lay trembling next to the china diver that had got rooted in there over the years? I told you to keep away from the weed, but as usual you paid little attention and swam in and out of it, peeking at me through the side of the tank and no doubt laughing to yourself for the sheer pleasure you were having. Then afterwards you danced naked on your towel till you were dry, clapping your hands. I can still hear your hands, clapping.

The thing was, you were so beautiful. I was always looking for excuses to be alone so that I could open your pouch and look at you curled up there. Anybody could have pinched your life out with a finger, but you lay there so much alive with a life of your own, so much taken up with your own dreams or your full warm stomach or the feel of my skin against your hands that I could never think of you as defenceless.

It's not ordinary beauty I'm talking about, anyway. How could you fail to have fine features, even though you took after me with my red cheeks and my black eyebrows that nearly meet over my nose? Nothing frightened you. You hadn't got a chance, really, if you'd only known it, but you got by because you refused to know it, and often I would just burst out laughing for joy at your boldness. What age do babies learn to climb? I suppose they don't climb a lot, in the usual way, but you climbed everywhere. Up my openwork vest. In and out of my front-fastening bra. And my hair! – you couldn't leave it alone. The day I made a plait and you went up it hand-over-hand until you reached my parting and you were so close to my ear I could hear you breathing hard and egging yourself on. I had a hand cupped under you all the time.

All this time you were reaching out, I was closing myself away. There was a job I would have killed for the year before, playing piano for a music therapist in a unit for handicapped children, but I had to turn it down. You were three by then, and I couldn't trust you to keep out of sight. By four you were learning, and at five I could take you anywhere and you'd lie still against me or I'd feel your body vibrating with laughter as you peered out through the gap in my blouse. What a sight I was! Loose blouses, sensible dresses with collars and plenty of pleats down the front. My sister Claire burst out once:

'For God's sake, Teresa, will you look at yourself in the mirror? It's the middle of July, why don't you put on your shorts and a sun-top like you used to? You're only thirty-one and anybody would think you were forty!' She was quite right. I looked older. Men didn't whistle or call after me in the streets any more as they'd been doing since I was twelve years old. I could wander along with my face up to the sun, and if my lips moved, nobody seemed to pay any attention. I think I must have had that look some women get when they're well on in pregnancy, inward and a bit taken up with something all the time. And that's a look which makes people leave you alone.

Did Matt know about you, or didn't he? Often, again and again, I'd think he'd seen you. I'd think maybe he played with you and talked to you and never let on for fear that once the whole business was out in the open we would have to do something about you. People would come to the house and tell us that arrangements ought to be made for you. You needed protection; a safe place maybe where you could be kept well away from things which would do you harm. Somewhere light and clean and airy with a spy-hole so that you could be kept an eye on. A little box for you.

You were ten years old and five inches tall. You ran fast, and you jumped high and when you skipped your feet didn't seem to touch the ground. Size for size, I'm sure you were quicker and nimbler than other children. When I looked closely at your feet I saw how strongly made they were, with high arches and long toes so you could climb and judge a distance and leap without ever making a mistake.

No, of course you made mistakes, Annina. Remember when my worst fear was realized and a cat got into the garden while I had my back turned to you, weeding. And you put out your fist to it and hit it on the nose as hard as you could so that it sprang back and cowered by the bird table, but not without giving you a slash on your forearm which was like a rip in silk. And it wanted stitching, but I couldn't think of anybody I could trust to do it, so I bound it tightly with the edges of the wound together and dressed it every day until it healed. You were lucky. It healed with only a faint white scar. Though you hated the scar, Annina, however much I told you it was hardly visible.

'You don't see it in the way I do,' you said, and of course you were right.

I thought the cat would have made you more cautious, but it was from then on that you began to go out on your own. You bound waxed thread around the eyelet of a darning-needle, and wore it at your side like a sword. You learned that cats would back off if you screamed at a certain pitch.

Blaise was at college, studying mathematics. When he came home he bent down to me and I kissed his fair prickly cheek with its big pores and splashed freckles and I thought of his sister out there in the jungle with her darning-needle. The bigness of Blaise's hand as he took his cup of coffee. His huge trainers kicked off and lying like mountains on the lino.

Annina, did you love Blaise, your brother? You knew more about him than I ever did. You stayed for hours in his room, listening to tapes with him, watching him study, hearing him talk to his friends. You knew what I didn't know, you heard what only came to me as a drone through the walls. My brother, you always said. 'Do you think my brother will be home soon? Are you making those sandwiches for my brother?'

Your light clear voice and your breath at the curve

of my ear. You liked best to talk perched up on my shoulder when I was moving about the house, cooking or tidying, or just sitting with a cup of coffee and an unread newspaper in front of me. And I learned to talk very lightly and quietly too, not whispering because that blurred the sounds too much for your ears. And never shouting, for too much noise made you tremble and curl up on yourself. The only thing that always made you afraid.

Annina, you know and I know that I could go on writing to you for ever, just as I could have listened to you for ever as you tucked your right arm round a curl of my hair and leaned yourself comfortably into the shape of my shoulder and told me things I had never seen and would never have been able to imagine. For we didn't really live in the same world, even though we shared house and home and bed and you shared my body as much as you needed it.

You went away and I have no one else who can talk of you. No one else knew you, no one else misses you or grieves for you. No one else would even believe in you.

You were so sure there were others like you, right from when you were a little girl.

'Have you ever told anybody about me?' you demanded. 'Well then! Nobody does! They all keep it secret, just like you do, for fear of what might happen. We need to find each other. How can I stay here knowing that somewhere in the world there are people like me, people of my own?'

You were like me, Annina. You looked like me. I think

even our skins and our hair smelled the same. But that was no good to you, and even though I longed for you to stay more than I had ever longed for anything, I made you a pair of trousers and a jacket from buckskin I got from a child's cowboy and Indian outfit, and I bought thermal silk for your leggings and vests, and you made your own shoes as you had had to learn to do, for I could never get the stitching small enough, and it bruised your feet.

My son went to college with a trunkful of books and a cake I'd made and a letter a week and a telephone in his hall of residence. He went with a bank account and the name of a doctor and his dental records up to date and his term's fees paid. He went with a pair of National Health glasses for reading and vaccination marks on his arm. He went with both of us waving from the station platform and his father slipping him a fiver to get himself something decent to eat on the train.

It was no good giving Annina money. Where and how could she spend it? My daughter went with a backpack on her back which we'd designed together after hours of thought and cutting the silk into the wrong shapes. Light and tough, that was what she wanted. She went with food and drink and I have to say she went with a great gift for stealing, which I hoped would stand her in good stead when she grew cold and hungry out in the world. She went with her darning-needle sword at her side, and a sleeping-bag filled with the finest down which I'd snipped from duck breast feathers. My daughter went very quickly, slipping through a hole in the fence, following a map of holes and gaps and secrets and hiding-places which she knew and I did not.

I've learned your language, Annina, and now I've no one to speak it with. So I'm still talking to you, wherever you are. It's all right to listen, Annina, for I'm not saying any words that might weaken you. I'm willing you on, Annina, morning and evening. I'll never so much as whisper *'Come home.'*

POCKET PENGUINS

POCKET PENGUINS